# Surfing the Moon

Written by Emily Dodd

Illustrated by Omar Aranda and Ilias Arahovitis

## Collins

My name is Jack. I am ten years old.

It's Tuesday. I'm at school.

I don't like school because it smells like milk.

I've drawn the Moon in the top right-hand corner of my jotter. I will do this every day for a month to make a flicker book.

Every night I will look out at the Moon. The next day I will draw what I saw in my jotter. Every Moon will be a slightly different shape to the one before.

Did you know that it takes the Moon a month to orbit Earth?

The word "month" comes from the word "Moon". So I think we should call it a moonth.

Yesterday, when our teacher asked us what month it was, I shouted, "Don't you mean MOONTH?"

Everyone except the teacher laughed.

I started to tell the teacher why she should say MOONTH, but she said, "If you have something to say, Jack, you must put up your hand."

So I put up my hand.

"Yes, Jack?" said the teacher.

"I would like everybody to say moonth instead of month," I said.

The teacher didn't say anything for a very long time. Then she sighed and said, "No, Jack."

I knew that the teacher didn't mean, "No, Jack, we can't say moonth instead of month." She meant, "Be quiet, Jack."

Sometimes the best bit of school is when the bell rings and I can go home.

Granny and Grandad were there when
I got home.

I told Granny she was looking very wrinkly, and
Grandad's face went bright red. He stood up and
shouted that they were leaving. He looked at me as
if I was making a terrible smell.

Mum said, "Let's all have a cup of tea, shall we?"

But I shouted, "No! I'm leaving too!" and I ran to
my room.

I sat on my bed. I wished I hadn't shouted.
Sometimes words fly out of my mouth like a rocket.
I wish they didn't because people don't like
my words. And that means they don't like me.

I think Granny and Mum still like me, most of
the time.

Grandad sometimes likes me.

I know I'm different from other kids.

Granny knocked on my door and sat on my bed.

"I didn't mean to shout," I said.

"Grandad is grumpy," said Granny. "That's not your fault."

I told her I liked her wrinkles because they make smiley shapes on her face even when she's not smiling.

Granny said that was one of the nicest things anyone had ever said to her.

At supper, Grandad said, "I'm glad we stayed for
a meal. This food is delicious."

Maybe he was grumpy because he was hungry?

Grandad asked me about my day at school.
"Did you play with your friends?" he asked.
"Football? Games? Racing?"

Other kids play football together. Other kids play
games together. Other kids race each other.

"No," I said.

That night I looked out at the Moon. It is important to remember its shape so that I can draw it accurately in my jotter the next day.

I know a lot about the Moon.

It is 400 times smaller than the Sun.

The Moon pulls at Earth and Earth pulls at the Moon. That pull is called gravity. And gravity makes the earth bulge and the tides go in and out, every single day. It's an invisible force.

If I could surf, I would be riding on a wave
that's being pulled on the tide by the Moon.

I like that idea.

Mum and I watch the surfers at
the bay nearby. It looks hard because they all
fall off their surfboards a lot.

The next morning, I told Mum I needed to learn
to surf.

She checked her phone while I ate breakfast.
"There's a Surf School starting this Friday evening.
You'll have a Surf Buddy and meet lots of
new friends."

I wanted to learn to surf, but when I thought
about those other kids, my tummy hurt. "What if
the other kids don't like me?" I asked.

"Once you've got your wetsuit on, you'll be just
like everybody else," said Mum.

But I am not like everybody else. Even in a wetsuit. Sometimes this makes me sad. Or it can make me mad.

Mum says to count to ten, and then punch a pillow, when I'm feeling mad.

But then I imagined standing on a surfboard, catching an imaginary gravity rope pulled by the Moon, and the pain in my tummy turned into a nice fizzy feeling.

Friday came fast. I had tummy ache on the way to Surf School.

The instructor introduced me to my Surf Buddy. His name is Sam, and he has a big smile. "Do you like high fives?" he asked.

I told him that there are different names for the Moon, depending on its shape. "A new Moon, waxing Moon, gibbous Moon, full Moon and a crescent Moon."

"Wow!" said Sam. "You're a Moon expert, Jack." When he held his hand up for a high five, I high fived him right back.

All the other kids were talking to their Surf Buddies too. I didn't look at them. But I could hear there was quite a bit of high fiving going on.

Sam gave me a wetsuit. "It's a bit like a spacesuit," he said.

"Has it an oxygen supply, and will it protect me from lethal gamma rays?" I asked.

"No," Sam admitted. "But it will keep you warm in the water."

I did not like the feel of the wetsuit. I did not like the smell of the wetsuit. I did not like the look of the wetsuit. I did not want to put on the wetsuit.

I looked round. Most of the other kids were putting on their wetsuits.

I hated pulling the wetsuit up my legs. I hated pulling the wetsuit up to my armpits.

It was cold and wet and tight. It smelt weird.

"It warms up once you're in the water,"
Sam explained. "It traps a layer of warm water next
to your body."

I pushed my arms inside. The zip up the back
had a pull cord. When I pulled it up, I was ready.

"Now you look like a surfer," Sam said.

The instructor asked us to take our surfboards to the sand.

I told Sam that I didn't want to go into the water.

"Would you rather play football?" he asked.

I had to think about that because I am not very good at football. But I decided that I was wearing these weird wetsuit boots, so nobody would expect me to be good. "OK," I said.

Sam explained that the first bit of the surf lesson would be on dry land.

"After we've done this bit, we'll play football," he whispered.

We laid on our tummies on the surfboards and practised paddling. Then, when the instructor shouted "Jump!" we had to jump up and stand on our boards. That was hard but Sam said I did well.

The others took their surfboards into the water,
to practise paddling and standing up on them there.
There was a lot of splashing and squealing.
They did their best, but they weren't very good.

Sam and I played football. I wasn't very good.

"Tell me your favourite Moon fact," said Sam.

I told him what Neil Armstrong said when he stepped onto the Moon in 1969. *"That's one small step for a man, one giant leap for mankind."*

Then some of the kids came to join in with our game of football. At first, I didn't like that, but soon I loved it.

Nobody laughed at me or called me names. And I didn't laugh at them or shout out.

I had the best time.

I could see Mum waiting by the car. I couldn't wait to tell her all about Surf School.

But I didn't want to take off my wetsuit.

"Sorry, Jack," said Sam. "But we need to wash it for tomorrow's surfing class."

I started peeling it off very slowly. "Bye, Sam."

"Bye, Jack, see you next week!" We gave each other a high five.

I ran to the car.

"Did you have a good time?" asked Mum.

"I had a brilliant time!" I told her.

"Did the wetsuit smell funny?"

"It did, but I got used to it," I shouted. "I had the best time I've had all moonth!"

I couldn't wait for the next Friday to come.

Every night, I looked out at the Moon and the next day I drew what I saw in my jotter.

"I've drawn a full Moon week!" I shouted out on Tuesday. I didn't mean to. Everyone in the class turned and looked at me.

"Thank you, Jack," said the teacher. "I hope that means you've finished your Maths pages too?"

Everyone except me laughed.

I feel like the Moon sometimes. When kids laugh at me, it's like a space rock hits me hard and leaves a crater.

I wish I was more like the Earth. When rocks hit Earth, it recycles them into a layer of solid rock. I wish I had a layer of rock-hard protection.

Mum made me a sandwich before Surf School. "It's a Surf Snack," she said. "It'll give you lots of energy for surfing."

"Or playing football," I said.

When we got to Surf School, I ran up to Sam and we high fived.

I didn't mind pulling on my wetsuit this time. I knew it would warm up.

We had a beach lesson first. Jumping and standing on our surfboards.

Soon it was time to carry our surfboards to
the sea. Sam and I kept walking and talking. I was
enjoying our conversation so much that the cold
sea didn't stop my feet; I kept walking. I told him
more fascinating facts about the Moon.

Once the water was up to our chests, we counted
to three, and then we all ducked underwater.

It felt colder than I was expecting. But I liked it, even though there was water dripping down my neck after I came up.

"Good job!" said Sam.

I felt so brave that I dived onto the board, but I fell straight off the other side. Water went up my nose. I did not like that.

"I'll hold the board steady," said Sam.
"Now jump on."

I could feel the waves being pulled by the Moon,
lapping beneath me.

"That's one small step for a man, and one giant
leap for Jack-kind," said Sam.

I didn't want to lift my hands from the board
to high five, but I smiled because he had said just
the right thing.

"Are you ready to surf?" asked Sam.

I nodded.

"When I say 'Go!', start paddling and let the waves carry you."

It wasn't easy.

On the third time, when I started paddling, the wave suddenly caught me and carried me forwards. I was moving so fast, I felt like a shark. I was scared and excited at the same time.

When the surfboard reached the beach, I could hear everybody clapping.

Sam ran towards me. "You caught your first wave!" he said, and I rolled sideways off the board into the shallow water and we high fived.

Now I knew what it felt like to be pulled by an invisible gravity rope from the Moon.

"Again!" I shouted. "Let's go again!"

Sam and I pulled my surfboard back out to deeper water.

I got on and Sam shouted "Go!" I paddled but I couldn't catch another wave.

"I can't do this!" I shouted and I punched the sea. It made a big splash.

"It's the waves, it's not you, Jack," said Sam. He looked out to sea. "This one looks good. Go!"

I paddled hard and, all of
a sudden, I caught the wave!
I raised my arm to catch
an imaginary gravity rope
from the Moon. But that made
the surfboard wobble, and
before I could think what to do,
it had tipped me off forwards
and underwater...

... twirling, twisting, cold
and upside-down. I had never
felt so scared in my life.

My arms and legs were punching through
the water, trying to find a way out. I felt the board
hit my back.

Which way was up? Which way was down?

Suddenly, my toes touched the sand. I pushed
hard and broke through the surface of the water,
gasping and spluttering.

"I've got you," said Sam. He took my hand.

"I thought I was drowning," I whispered. I was trying not to cry.

"I wouldn't let that happen," said Sam. "I'm your Surf Buddy, remember?"

I pulled my hand away. "You're a bad Surf Buddy!" I shouted.

Later on, Sam told Mum what had happened. I jumped into the car and locked the door.

"I don't want to talk about it, and I'm never going back!" I shouted.

That night I looked out at the Moon.

I didn't want to think about gravity, or about the way the Moon pulled the waves. I didn't want to think about being underwater, wet, cold and the wrong way up.

Mum came and sat on my bed. "Sam said you were very brave," she said.

I thought about how amazing it had felt to catch that first wave. It was one of the best feelings I'd ever had. But I decided not to tell Mum about it.

"I'm not going back to Surf School," I said. "Not ever."

Two Fridays passed. I did not go to Surf School on either of those Fridays.

And then a new girl called Jess joined our class. I remembered her from Surf School. She always wore a purple beanie, and she wasn't very good at football.

She remembered me catching a wave. "Jack was brilliant," she told everyone. "You should have seen him surfing. He went so fast!"

The teacher looked rather surprised. "Well, Jack," she said. "Perhaps you'd like to tell us all about your surfing at Circle Time on Monday morning."

I asked Mum if she'd take me back to Surf School that Friday.

When we got there, Jess was there too.

"Great to see you, Jack," said Sam. He didn't high five me, but he gave me a big smile.

I pulled on the wetsuit, and Sam and I carried the surfboard to the edge of the water.

"Are you ready to catch a wave? Do you remember what to do?" Sam asked.

"Of course, he does," said Jess. "Jack is a brilliant surfer!"

We floated the surfboard out to sea.
Then we waited. And we waited. It needed to be just the right wave.

But I kept remembering what it had felt like to be underwater and not know which way was up or down. I kept remembering the water in my ears, and up my nose.

"I don't want to surf today," I said.

Sam and I towed the surfboard back to the shore.

I sat on the sand and watched Jess catching wave after wave after wave.

On Monday morning, I told the teacher
that I wouldn't be talking about surfing.
But I did explain about my flicker book. I had
34 Moons now. A whole month and four days.
I didn't mention moonths.

"Thank you, Jack," said the teacher, smiling.

At lunch, I asked Jess about surfing.

"I feel scared," said Jess. "But I allow myself
to let go and feel wobbly for that one moment as
I stand. It's like there's an invisible force you get
past and then it's easy after that. If you take a risk
to stand, you'll realise you can do it."

I nodded.

"And you'll go under lots of times. It's called
a wipe out. I've had loads of them. But I always
come back up and try again, that's how I learnt
to surf."

That Friday I went back to
Surf School.

"Hello, Sam," I said, and we
high fived.

I pulled on my wetsuit, and we
carried the surfboard to the water.

"Let's catch a wave," said Sam.

And we did.

I didn't need Sam to say "Go!",
I just needed to choose the best wave
possible and paddle hard.

Every time I caught a wave,
I rode it on my tummy. I could hear
claps and cheers and whistles as
I landed at the beach. I just needed
to try to stand up, like Jess said.

And on the last wave of
the evening, I did it, I stood up, just
for three seconds but I did it. I was
a real surfer. Mum was there too.
And so were Granny and Grandad.

Grandad was cheering louder
than anybody else.

It's bedtime. I'm looking at the Moon again.

Tomorrow I will draw the fortieth Moon in my jotter! I will flick through all 40 pages and I will watch the Moon change shape as it orbits Earth.

But before I do that, I'm going to do something new. I will draw a surfer on the last full Moon.

I will call that surfer Jack.

The surfer will remind me of how I learnt to do something hard and scary by conquering an invisible force. This invisible force isn't to do with the Moon. It's an invisible force that stops you doing things, called fear.

You can beat it, with another force that's stronger than fear. It's a force called courage.

# Conquering fear

# Ideas for reading

Written by Gill Matthews
*Primary Literacy Consultant*

**Reading objectives:**
- draw inferences such as inferring characters' feelings, thoughts and motives from their actions, and justify inferences with evidence
- participate in discussion about both books that are read to them and those they can read for themselves, taking turns and listening to what others say

**Spoken language objectives:**
- articulate and justify answers, arguments and opinions
- give well-structured descriptions, explanations and narratives for different purposes, including for expressing feelings

**Curriculum links:** Relationships education – the characteristics of friendships, including mutual respect, truthfulness, trustworthiness, loyalty, kindness, generosity, trust, sharing interests and experiences and support with problems and difficulties.

Relationships education – the importance of respecting others, even when they are very different from them (for example, physically, in character, personality or backgrounds), or make different choices or have different preferences or beliefs.

**Interest words:** conquering, invisible, force, courage

## Build a context for reading

- Ask children to look at the front cover and to read the title. Explore what they think *Surfing the Moon* might mean. Check that children are familiar with what surfing entails.

- Read the back-cover blurb. Explain that the different ways people's brains work is called *neurodiversity*. Establish that this is a contemporary story so it takes place in the present time.

- Ask children what they think might happen in the story. Encourage them to support their predictions with reasons.

## Understand and apply reading strategies

- Read pp2–9 aloud to the children. Ask who is telling the story. Explore how the children feel about Jack and the things he says in the story. What do they think about Grandad's reaction? Encourage children to support their responses with reasons and evidence from the text.